PJMASKS

Time to Be a Hero

Based on the screenplay
"Blame It on the Train, Owlette"

Ready-to-Read

Simon Spotlight
New York   London   Toronto   Sydney   New Delhi

SIMON SPOTLIGHT
An imprint of Simon & Schuster Children's Publishing Division
1230 Avenue of the Americas, New York, New York 10020
This Simon Spotlight edition November 2016
This book is based on the TV series PJ MASKS © Frog Box / Entertainment One UK
Limited / Walt Disney EMEA Productions Limited 2014; Les Pyjamasques by Romuald ©
(2007) Gallimard Jeunesse. All Rights Reserved.
This book/publication © Entertainment One UK Limited 2016.
Adapted by Daphne Pendergrass from the series PJ Masks
All rights reserved, including the right of reproduction in whole or in part in any form.
SIMON SPOTLIGHT, READY-TO-READ, and colophon are registered trademarks of
Simon & Schuster, Inc.
For information about special discounts for bulk purchases, please contact
Simon & Schuster Special Sales at 1-866-506-1949 or business@simonandschuster.com.
Manufactured in the United States of America 0518 LAK
10 9
ISBN 978-1-4814-8648-4 (hc)
ISBN 978-1-4814-8647-7 (pbk)
ISBN 978-1-4814-8649-1 (eBook)

The train is gone!

Connor, Amaya, and Greg
are at the fair.
"I want to ride the train!"
Amaya says.
But where is it?

The PJ Masks can find it!

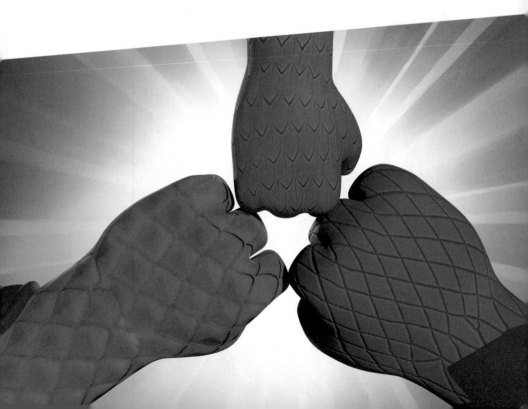

Greg becomes Gekko!

Connor becomes Catboy!

Amaya becomes Owlette!

They are the PJ Masks!

Owlette really wants
to ride the train.

She is in a rush
to find it.

Owlette jumps into
the Cat-Car.

"Come on!" she says.

She uses her Owl Eyes
to see far away.

Owlette sees the train!

Romeo is driving it!

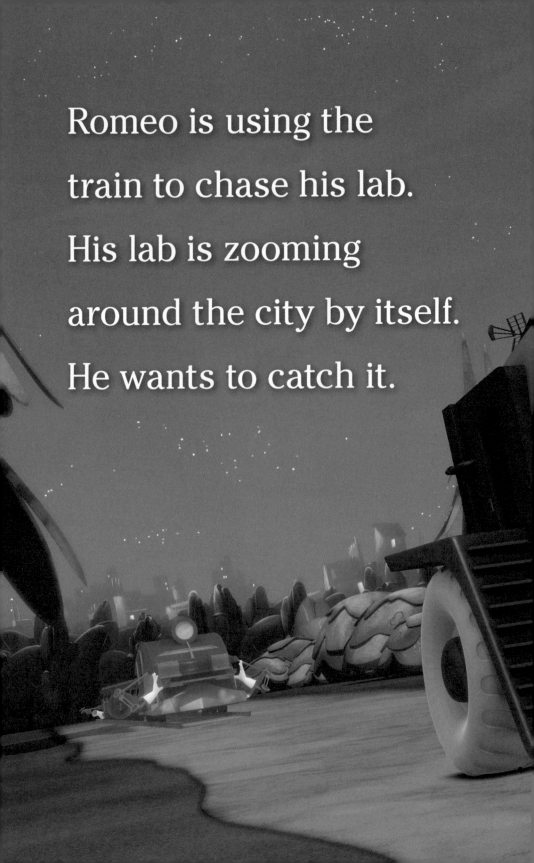

Romeo is using the train to chase his lab. His lab is zooming around the city by itself. He wants to catch it.

The PJ Masks jump

onto the train!

Owlette rushes ahead
to stop Romeo.

"Wait for us!" Gekko
and Catboy say.
Romeo catches Owlette!

Gekko and Catboy

help her escape.

"I am sorry," Owlette says. "I should have listened and not rushed. It is time to be a hero!"

Owlette has a plan.
The PJ Masks will
work together.

Catboy gathers
some branches.
He throws them to Owlette.

Gekko climbs onto the train.

Owlette throws the
branches to Gekko.
He jams the train tracks
with them!

The train is out of control.

Gekko is very strong.

He stops the train.

The train cars swing around the lab and trap it.

Romeo leaves the train.

He is so happy to have

his lab back.

PJ Masks all shout hooray!

Because in the night,

we saved the day!

The PJ Masks return
the train to the fair.
The day is saved!